DAVEY PANDA

God Didn't Give You the Spirit of Fear

AUGUST 17, 2019
MYRA G. LOVE MINISTRIES

Davey got excited when he heard the great news.

A visitor was coming but he wasn't sure who.

Dave said, "Mama who could it be?"

She smiled and said, "Just wait and see."

Davey did his chores that he was asked to do.

Mama said "After you're finished, tidy your bedroom too."

Later they went to the store to get things for the guest.
After everything was done, they were due for some rest.

The next morning there was a knock at the door.
Davey was happy that he didn't have to wait anymore.

Davey opened the door but didn't see anyone outside.
Cousin JoJo was hiding, then jumped out and yelled **"Surprise!"**

JoJo went in the house to put his things away.
After he was done, the boys went out to play.

The boys were running around and having lots of fun.

Davey saw a butterfly, he yelled and started to run.

When he got home, Mama asked, "Why did you run away?"
Davey said, "I saw a big bug and now I'm afraid to play."

Mama said,
"God didn't give the spirit of fear, but power, love and a sound mind.
When you're afraid, call on the Lord, He's with you every time."

The boys went to play and saw Cam climb the tree.

JoJo went to the top then heard Davey yell, "It's a beeeee!!!"

Davey ran so fast yelling all the way.
He got home and said "I'll never go out to play."

God didn't give you the spirit of fear, but power, love and a sound mind.
Just think of God when you're afraid, He's with you every time.

It was late so Cam called his Mom to see if he could stay.
Cam's Mom said "Yes" and the boys shouted **"Yayyyy!!!"**

The boys said their prayers and Mama and Papa said goodnight.
As they left the room Cam said "Please don't turn off the light."

Cam said, "I'm afraid of the dark and I can't sleep at all."
Davey said, "Let's pray to the Lord, He hears us when we call."

God didn't give you the spirit of fear, but power, love and a sound mind.

Call on the Lord when you're afraid, He's with you every time.

Cam felt much better and the boys fell fast asleep.

The boys slept so sound that you couldn't hear a peep.

The next day the boys went to play and they were having lots of fun.
A big spider went close to Davey but this time he didn't run.

Davey says, "God didn't give me the spirit of fear,
I'm not gonna run, I'm gonna stay right here.
"God gave me power, love and a sound mind.
I'm not afraid, God is with me every time."

The spider, the bee and butterfly all asked if they could play?

Davey, Cam and JoJo said "Yes" and they all enjoyed the day.

20

They laughed, played, sang songs and are now the best of friends.

Davey says, "He's your friend too and see you next time."

The End!

Davey's Corner

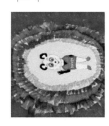

1. What was Davey afraid of?
2. How did Davey overcome his fear?
3. Can you remember what scripture Davey used?
4. Do you ever get afraid of something or someone?
5. If so what or who?
6. What can you do to overcome your fears?
7. What Person can you talk to about your fears?

Davey wants you to say: 2 Timothy 1: 7 (KJV)

For God hath not given us the spirit of fear; but of power, and of love, and of a sound mind.

Draw your favorite character from this book.

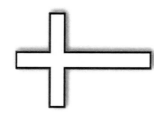

This book is dedicated to the Lord Jesus.

A Special thank you to all of my wonderful supporters.

May the Lord Bless you all now and forevermore!